D0516469

# I HAD A FAVORITE HAT

By
Boni Ashburn

Pictures by
Robyn Ng

Abrams Books for Young Readers
New York

For Carol,
who inspires me every day
—B.A.

For Mom, Dad, and Evelyn,
with all my love
—R.N.

The art for this book was made with graphite, watercolor, pencil crayon, ink, needle and thread, cut paper, Photoshop, and the love of friends and family.

Library of Congress Cataloging-in-Publication Data
Ashburn, Boni.
I Had a Favorite Hat / by Boni Ashburn ; pictures by Robyn Ng.
pages cm
Summary: At the end of summer, a girl's mother wants to put away her favorite beach hat but the girl asks to keep it out, then decorates it for each holiday and season from autumn through spring.
ISBN 978-1-4197-1462-7
[1. Hats—Fiction. 2. Handicraft—Fiction. 3. Seasons—Fiction.]
I. Ng, Robyn, illustrator. II. Title.
PZ7.A7992Iak 2015
[E]—dc23
2014015762


Book design by Chad W. Beckerman with Robyn Ng



Printed and bound in China
10 9 8 7 6 5 4 3 2 1

115 West 18th Street
New York, NY 10011
www.abramsbooks.com

I had a favorite hat that was my bestest hat ever. I wore it every day at the beach to keep the sunny blue skies out of my eyes.

It was flippy...

and floppy...

. . . and

perfectly

sloppy!

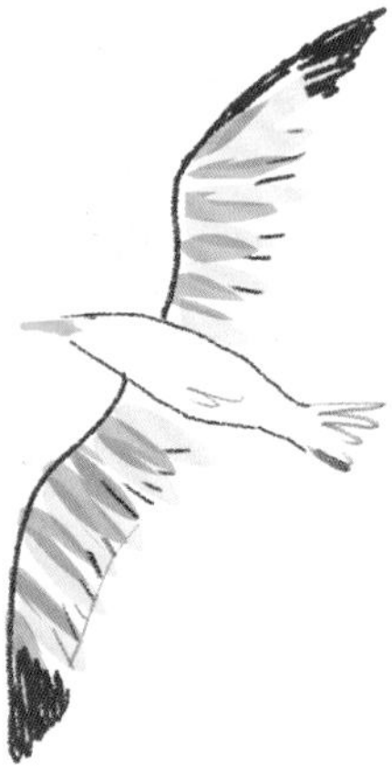

At the end of the summer, Mama packed up my beach things and said, “Bye until spring!” but I said, “Wait, wait, wait—not my hat!”

THIS WAY UP

"My dear," Mama said, "that hat is so *clearly* a beach hat! It just won't look right anywhere else."

But she was wrong—it could be so much more! I snatched my favorite hat from the Summery Things pile with a crafty smile, and it hung on my door, my favorite hat, waiting to be so much more . . .

When the crisp, cool days of autumn fell, Maggie Jean, my very bestest partner in crime, said, "What shall we be *this* time?" I was inspired!

With a little of **this**...

and a little of **that**...

I had the perfect **hat** for my Halloween costume! Aren't we a scream?!

When we took down the cobwebs and bats, Mama said, “Now the hat!” and I said, “Just like *that*? See how it’s *more* than a beach hat?”

I took off **this**,

and I took off **that**,

and I hung it back on my door once more . . .

Until Mrs. Campbell sang out one day, in her singsong way, "For Holiday Concert Night, wear what feels just right!" I tried and tried but couldn't decide, until Maggie Jean eyed my favorite hat—which *always* feels just right!

With a little of **this**...

and a little of **that**...

I had an oh-so-cozy, here-comes-the-snow **hat**
that felt just right while we sang our holiday songs.

After the happy holidays, we boxed up the holly, but I grabbed my hat back. “Not yet!” I said, because it occurred to me that . . .

with a little of **this** . . .

and a little of **that** . . .

I had the perfect Birthday Girl hat for me! I wore my hat for all to see while I blew out *all* the candles in one big . . .

whoooooosh!

I'm another whole year older now, but I still play dress-up with Maggie Jean, the Fashion Queen. You're never too old to play dress-up.

And with a little of **this** . . .

and a little of **that** . . .

my not-just-a-beach-**hat** looks oh-so-right with my favorite dress-up dress. Who knew?

Mama says, with a sigh and misty eyes, "You look just like Eliza Doolittle!" and Maggie Jean and I reply, "Eliza WHO-little?!" because we think just alike, don't you know, and we don't even *know* who that is! Mama mutters something about fairs and ladies while Maggie Jean and I finish our fashion show.

"Everything back in the trunks!" is the rule, but my hat is too cool to put back! I sneak it past Mama and stash it on top of my red swingy sweater.

When I pull out my sweater on Valentine's Day, I say, "Hey!" and . . .

With a little of **this**. . .

and a little of **that**. . .

. . . my **hat** makes a divine little valentine!

Even Henry Stevens thinks so . . .

Until he doesn't. *Sigh*. Wise Maggie Jean says, "Heartbreak? Pshaw . . . Let's make something new, so you don't feel blue!" We look at my calendar and find the perfect thing on it!

With a little of **this**...

and a little of **that**...

An Easter bonnet! Maggie Jean and I look sweet as treats (Mama said so, you know) and oh-so-grown-up, with the tiny little heels on the shoes on our feet. Not too grown-up for an egg hunt, though! And you're never too old for jelly beans.

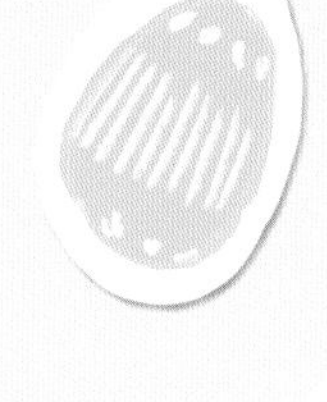

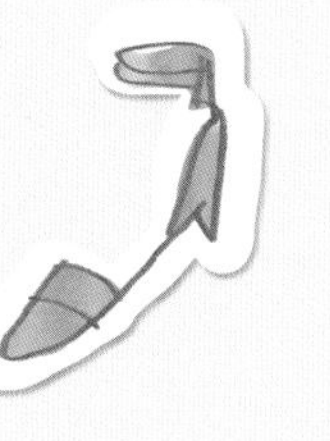

Then I unmake my bonnet till there's nothing on it—again.

One day at Grandma's house, with the green-on-green, fence-to-fence lawn, we decide to start a garden.

"Lovely," says Grandma, and we weed, wait, and watch, day after day, until . . .

pop! pop!
pop!

Up they sprout!

But wait a minute.

"GET
OUT!"

“I know just the thing!” Grandma sings. We cut and staple and stuff till our scarecrow seems scary and tough. But does he have the right stuff? No, he doesn’t.

So I add on my hat, my favorite **hat** . . .

with a little of **this**...

and a little of **that**...

and it flappity-flaps in the breeze.

He makes it look easy all spring, don't you know, as he scares away every last single crow, and our garden grows leafy and green.

But one windy Wednesday,
my hat,
just like that, flew away!
Grandma said so.

And now there
was nothing left
of my dear,
departed hat.
Oh no!

At the beach, I tell my sad hat story to Maggie Jean as I try in vain to keep the sunny blue skies out of my eyes.

“No worries!” says my unflappable friend, reaching into her beach bag. “Floppy-sloppy hats are *o-u-t* anyway. Trim, shiny visors are in!”

I'm not so sure that my new hat is a win, but I *do* know . . .

with a little of **this** . . . and a little of **that** . . .

my new **hat** can be anything I want it to be!